KV-683-961

HANS CHRISTIAN ANDERSEN

THE OLD HOUSE

ILLUSTRATED BY JEAN CLAVERIE

Translated and adapted by Anthea Bell

On the other side of the street there stood an old, old house. It was almost three hundred years old; the date was carved on the balcony, among tulips and vine tendrils. The upper floor of the house stuck out above the lower one.

The other buildings in the street were smart and new. You could see they wanted nothing to do with the old house. They probably wondered: how long is that ramshackle old place going to stand here? Its turret blocks the view, the iron banisters of the steps up to it might be leading to some old tomb, and they have brass knobs on too! What a sight!

The houses opposite were smart and new as well, and they thought just the same. But a little boy with fresh, rosy cheeks and bright, shining eyes used to sit at one of their windows.

He liked the old house best of all, in sunlight or in moonlight, and when he looked across at the peeling plaster of its walls he could see the street just as it used to be, with steps and turrets and pointed gables.

An old man lived in the old house. He wore knee breeches, a coat with big brass buttons, and a wig. There was an old manservant who used to come to tidy up and run his errands every morning, but apart from that he lived alone.

Now and then he came to his window and looked out, and the little boy nodded to him, and he nodded back, and so they came to be friends without ever exchanging a word.

One day the little boy heard his parents say, "The old man over the road is very well off, but dreadfully lonely." So next Sunday he wrapped something in a piece of paper and went down to the front door. When the old manservant came by, he asked, "Please, would you take this to the old man opposite? I have two tin soldiers and I want to give him one, because I know he's lonely."

So the tin soldier was taken across the road, and an invitation came back for the little boy to go and visit the old man himself. His parents gave him permission, so he went over.

The brass knobs on the banisters shone as if they had been polished up specially for his visit, and the trumpeters who were carved standing in the tulips on the door seemed to be blowing for all they were worth, puffing out their cheeks. "Tantantara! Here comes the little boy, tantantara!"

The hall of the old house was hung with portraits of knights in armour and ladies in silken gowns. The armour clinked and the gowns rustled. You went a long way up a staircase, and a little way down, and then you were on a balcony. It was very fragile, with holes and cracks in the floor, but green grass and leaves grew out of all the cracks so that it looked like a garden. There were old flower pots here, with faces and big ears. One pot was full of pinks, or rather of their green shoots, and it said, quite distinctly,

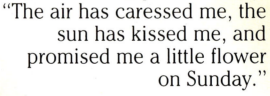

"The air has caressed me, the sun has kissed me, and promised me a little flower on Sunday."

There was a room whose walls were covered with pigskin stamped with golden flowers.

"*When gilding is past,*
  pigskin will last,"
said the walls.

The chairs had tall, carved backs and arms. "Sit down!" they said. "Sit down! Oh dear, how I creak! I'm getting rheumatics, like the old cupboard!"

The little boy went into the room with the turret, where the old man sat. "Thank you for the tin soldier, my little friend," said the old man. "And thank you for coming to see me!"

"Thanks! Thanks!" or, "Creak! Creak!" said all the furniture.

There was a picture of a beautiful lady on one wall. She was young and happy, but she wore stiff, old-fashioned clothes, and had powder in her hair. She did not say "Thanks!" or "Creak!" but looked kindly at the little boy.

"Oh, where did you get her?" he asked the old man.

"From the junk shop," said the old man. "It's full of pictures that nobody cares for, because the people in them are dead, but I knew that lady long ago. She has been dead and gone for half a century now."

There was a bunch of withered flowers behind glass underneath the picture. They looked as if they had been dead for half a century too.

"They say at home that you're dreadfully lonely," said the little boy.

"Oh," said the old man, "old thoughts visit me, with all they can bring, and now you are here too, so I do very well."

Then he took a picture book off the shelf. It showed processions of strange, old-fashioned carriages, soldiers dressed like the Knave of Clubs, and tradesmen carrying streaming banners. The tailors' banner showed two lions holding a pair of scissors, and the cobblers' banner showed an eagle with two heads. What a picture book that was!

The old man went into the next room to fetch sweetmeats and apples and nuts. It was really lovely over here in the old house.

"I can't stand it!" said the tin soldier, standing on a cabinet. "It's so sad and lonely here! I can't stand it! It's not a bit like your home over the road, with your mother and father talking so happily, and you and all the other dear children having such fun! The old man is so lonely! Do you think he gets kisses, or kind looks, or a Christmas tree? All he'll ever get is a funeral! I can't stand it!"

"But you must!" said the little boy. "Don't take it so hard! I think it's lovely here, and old thoughts will visit you, with all they can bring!"

Then the old man came back with some delicious sweetmeats and apples and nuts, and the little boy forgot the tin soldier. He went home feeling very happy.

Days went by, and weeks went by, and the little boy visited the old man again. The carved trumpeters blew, the armour clinked, the silk gowns rustled, the pigskin talked, and all the chairs had rheumatics.

It was all just like his first visit, for one day was the same as another in the old house.

"I can't stand it!" said the tin soldier. "I've been weeping tin tears. It's too sad here. I'd rather go to war and lose my arms and legs – at least that would make a change! I can't stand it! I've had visits from my own old thoughts, and believe me, that's no fun. I nearly jumped off this cabinet the other day. I seemed to see all of you over the road, quite plain and clear. It was that Sunday morning when you children were singing a hymn as usual, with your hands folded, and your mother and father looking very solemn too, and the door opened and in came your little sister Maria, who isn't quite two and always dances when she hears any kind of music or singing. So she began to dance, but she couldn't get the time right, because the notes were so long. And I laughed so much that I fell off the table and dented my head. I still have the dent. Tell me, do you still sing on Sundays? Tell me about little Maria! And how is my comrade, the other tin soldier? He has all the luck! Oh, I can't stand it!"

"You were given away," said the little boy, "so you must stay. Can't you see that?"

When the old man came in with a
drawer full of wonderful things such as big,
gilded playing cards. He opened the piano
too. It had a picture painted inside the lid, and
it sounded hoarse when the old man played
it. He hummed a tune.

"She knew that song," he said, looking at
the portrait on the wall.

"I want to go to war!
I want to go to war!"
shouted the tin soldier
as loud as he could, and
he flung himself down
on the floor.

The old man looked
for him, and so did the
little boy, but he had
disappeared. "I'll find
him some time," said
the old man, but he nev-
er did, for the tin soldier
had fallen through a
crack in the floorboards,
and there he lay as if in
an open grave.

The day came to an end, and the little boy went home. That week passed by, and so did several more. The windows were all frozen up, and the little boy had to breathe on them to see through. Drifts of snow were blown into all the carvings on the old house, and snow covered its steps, as if there were no one at home. Nor was there, because the old man had died.

In the evening he was carried out of the door in his coffin, and taken away to lie in his grave in the country. No one followed the coffin, for all his friends were dead, but the little boy blew kisses after it as it was driven off.

There was a sale at the old house several days later. Sitting at his window, the little boy saw everything being taken away: the knights and ladies, the flower pots, the old chairs and cupboards. The portrait of the lady went back to the junk shop, and there it stayed, because no one knew her any more.

In spring the house itself was knocked down, and you could see right into the room with pigskin on its walls from the street. The pigskin was all tattered and torn.

Then everything was cleared away.

"Good riddance!" said the other houses.

Asplendid new house was built instead, with big windows and smooth white walls. And a little garden was planted in front of it, where the old house itself had once stood. Wild vines grew up the walls next door, and dozens of sparrows perched in them, chattering away, but not about the old house, which they could not remember.

Years passed by, and the little boy grew up to be a fine, tall man. He had just married, and moved into the house with the garden with his wife. He was standing beside her as she planted a wild flower, pressing the soil firm with her fingers.

"Oh – what was that?" She had pricked herself on something sharp sticking out of the ground.

Just imagine – it was the tin soldier who had been lost in the old man's house! He had been tumbled about in its timbers and rubble, and then he lay in the earth for years on end.

The young woman dried the tin soldier with a green leaf, and then with her fine, scented handkerchief, and he felt as if he were waking from a deep sleep.

"Let me see!" said the young man. He laughed, and shook his head. "It can't be the same one, but he reminds me of a tin soldier I had as a little boy." And he told his wife the whole story.

"Why, it may be the same tin soldier after all," she said. "I'll keep him, and you must show me the old man's grave."

"I don't know where it is," he said. "No one does. His friends were all dead, nobody tended it, and I was only a little boy."

"How dreadfully lonely he must have been!" she said.

"Dreadfully lonely!" said the tin soldier. "But it's good not to be forgotten."

"Yes, it's good!" cried something close by, but no one except the tin soldier saw that it was a scrap of pigskin from the old walls. It had lost all its gilding and looked like wet earth, but it still had its own opinion, which it gave.

"When gilding is past,
 pigskin will last,"
However, the tin soldier did not believe it.

Copyright © 1984 Nord-Süd Verlag, Mönchaltorf, Switzerland
First published under the title Das Alte Haus
English text copyright © 1984 Anthea Bell
First published in Great Britain 1984 under the imprint
Abelard/North-South by Abelard-Schuman Ltd
A Member of the Blackie Group
Furnival House, 14-18 High Holborn, London WC1V 6BX

All rights reserved

British Library Cataloguing in Publication Data
Andersen, H.C.
  The old house
  I. Title II. Claverie, Jean III. Bell. Anthea
  IV. Das alte Haus. *English*

839.8′1364 [J]   PZ8

ISBN 0-200-72853-9

Printed in Germany